STORIES OF

# SURVIVAL
# & REVENGE

FROM INUIT FOLKLORE

Published in Canada by Inhabit Media Inc. (www.inhabitmedia.com) • Inhabit Media Inc.

(Iqaluit Office), P.O. Box 11125, Iqaluit, Nunavut, X0A 1H0 • (Toronto Office), 146A Orchard View Blvd., Toronto, Ontario, M4R 1C3

Edited by Neil Christopher and Louise Flaherty • Written by Rachel and Sean Qitsualik-Tinsley • Illustrated by Jeremy Mohler

Design and layout copyright © 2015 Inhabit Media Inc. • Text copyright © 2015 by Rachel and Sean Qitsualik-Tinsley • Illustrations by Jeremy Mohler copyright © 2015 Inhabit Media Inc.

Printed and bound in Canada

We acknowledge the support of the Canada Council for the Arts for our publishing program.

We acknowledge the support of the Government of Canada through the Department of Canadian Heritage Canada Book Fund program.

Library and Archives Canada Cataloguing in Publication

Qitsualik-Tinsley, Rachel, 1953-, author
     Stories of survival & revenge from Inuit folklore / written
by Rachel & Sean Qitsualik-Tinsley ; illustrated by Jeremy
Mohler.

ISBN 978-1-77227-001-3 (pbk.)

     1. Inuit--Folklore--Comic books, strips, etc.  2. Graphic novels.
I. Qitsualik-Tinsley, Sean, 1969-, author  II. Mohler, Jeremy, illustrator
III. Title.  IV. Title: Stories of survival and revenge from Inuit folklore.

PN6733.Q58S76 2015              j741.5'971          C2015-900716-X

Canadian Heritage
Patrimoine canadien

Canada Council for the Arts
Conseil des Arts du Canada

# STORIES OF
# SURVIVAL
# & REVENGE
## FROM INUIT FOLKLORE

WRITTEN BY

RACHEL & SEAN QITSUALIK-TINSLEY

ILLUSTRATED BY

JEREMY MOHLER

# CONTENTS

# FOREWORD

Life in the Arctic can be difficult. Think about the cold, severe storms, shifting ice, and difficulty of finding food. Imagine the ingenuity required to hunt Arctic animals without much wood or metal to make weapons. Inuit depended on each other to survive in this northern world. Many Inuit customs and taboos were passed down to ensure that the relationships of a camp or village remained strong.

Even though life could be difficult and much knowledge needed to be learned, you will find that in Inuit elders rarely explained things directly. That was not the way. Instead, you were expected to watch, listen, and learn. Knowledge and wisdom were things each person earned on their own. And one of the ways that values were shared and passed on was through stories. Inuit culture is rich with stories. Many of the rules of life, and much of Inuit history, values, and beliefs are encoded in stories.

Inuit believed that knowledge was personal, and that each person's knowledge and understanding was unique and valuable. In this book you will read three cautionary tales told by two gifted storytellers. Consider each tale as you read it. What is the message? Why was this story told?

Even though the world has changed, you will find that these old stories still have much to teach us.

Neil Christopher & Louise Flaherty
*Iqaluit, Nunavut, 2015*

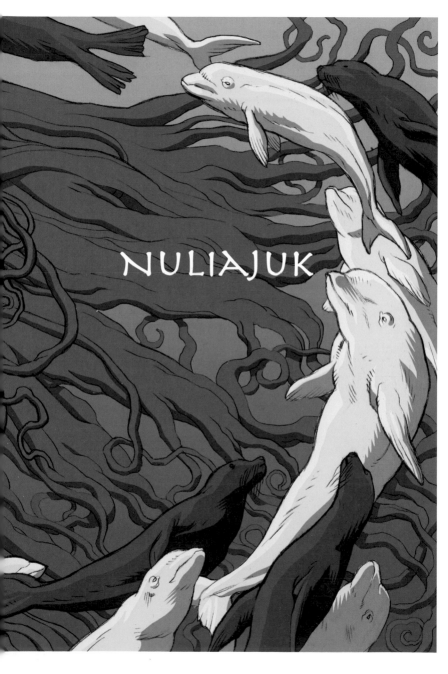

NULIAJUK

*In times long ago:*

There was a girl who lived only with her father and some dogs. She was pretty, so her father had guessed that he could easily find a husband for her. He was wrong.

Over and over again, young hunters came to visit the girl and her father. Each visitor asked if he could marry the girl. But she was rude. She ignored the hunters, or hid herself, until they grew frustrated and left. Her father grew angry.

"You have to marry someone, someday," he would tell her.

"Never," she would answer. Every time, she told her father, "I'll never marry."

There was a particular stone behind which the girl liked to hide when hunters came to visit. It was round, with red and white markings. One day, the girl reached out to touch it.

And it suddenly became a dog!

The girl hugged the magic dog. She loved it. She wanted to be near it all the time. And after while, she wanted to marry it.

Just as the girl's father could do nothing to make her marry a young hunter, he could not prevent her from marrying the dog. To her father's disgust, she was a wife to it in every way. In time, she even became pregnant by it.

The father stood helpless while his daughter gave birth to a litter of pups.

But they were far from normal young. They combined the features of dog and human being. Some were very doglike, walking on all fours, but having human faces. Others were almost like human beings, except that they were fierce and hairy.

The girl's father was so horrified by his new grandchildren that he immediately wanted to kill them and their dog-father. He managed to kill the dog, but his daughter cried for her half-human children to be spared. So her father let them live, though he made his daughter send them off to the far corners of the earth. In those faraway places, it is said, they became peoples other than the Inuit.

So the girl went back to living with her father and refusing to marry a human being. Always, whenever a young hunter arrived, she would give excuses like:

"He's too short."
"He's too fat."
"His eyes are ugly."
"His feet are strange."
"His clothes are poor."

One late summer, the girl was combing her hair near the water's edge. She looked up to see a *qajaq* approaching. The qajaq was paddled by a young man with perfect

features. His clothes were beautiful. He wore snow goggles across his eyes, so she could not see them—but the rest of his appearance greatly impressed her.

The young man left his qajaq on the shore and greeted the girl and her father. Sometime later, like so many young hunters before him, he asked if he could marry the girl. The girl's father slumped over, groaning, knowing that his daughter would refuse.

But this time, she shocked him. She looked at the young hunter and cried, "Yes!"

Happily, the old father watched as his daughter—finally married—left with her new husband.

The young couple travelled far. The girl talked along the way, but her husband was silent. She kept speaking. She asked him to say something. Anything. But he remained quiet.

In time, they arrived at a small island. It was covered in squawking, squabbling birds. Their droppings were everywhere, leaving smelly streaks and spatter marks on every stone.

The island turned the girl's stomach. She thought that maybe her new husband had made a mistake. Perhaps he needed to stop here for some reason. But the young hunter only pointed toward a beach on the bird-covered island, saying, "Home."

The girl squinted, looking at where he had pointed. Amid the larger stones of the beach, she could see a ragged tent, streaked with bird dung, like everything else on the island.

She stood in shock while watching her husband drag his qajaq up from the beach. Every few seconds, the wind shifted, carrying the stench of the tent toward her. She felt sick.

Her husband noticed her reaction.

He began to laugh.

"You don't like your new home?" he asked, his voice changing to something more like a bird's squawk. "Get used to it, girl. You're mine. And you're never leaving."

As he spoke, he removed the snow goggles from his eyes, which turned out to be red as blood. His body began to shift. To change. After a few moments, he revealed himself to be a petrel-spirit: a shape-changer that was half-human, half-bird, and all monster.

The girl screamed and screamed. She screamed for her father, for any human ears that might hear her.

But there was no answer, other than the monster's laughter.

The girl lived in misery after that. She lived in the filth and noise of that island. Her husband ordered the other birds to keep her alive. They brought her food— but only in a bird's way, vomiting up the small, often rotten fish that they picked up along the coasts.

Much time passed. The girl's father began to wonder why he was never visited by his daughter and new son-in-law. He became worried. Since he was a shaman, he sent out his helper-spirit to find his daughter. In the form of a bird, the helper flew up and down the coasts. Finally, it found the island where the girl was kept captive. The helper immediately flew back, telling the father what it had discovered.

When the father learned that his daughter had been kidnapped by a petrel-spirit, he thought long and hard. Though it was dangerous, he decided that he must rescue his foolish daughter.

Using his own qajaq, the father paddled to the island of the birds. His daughter saw him coming from a distance, and ran to meet him, tears streaming down her face.

The father glanced around nervously. He knew that the petrel-spirit was dangerous, and would not look kindly on having his new wife stolen away.

"Where is your husband?" the father asked.

"He's gone," said the girl, "for now."

"Then let's hurry," her father said.

Placing his daughter on the flat top of his qajaq, the father paddled away from the island. But they did not get far before the

girl, looking behind, let out a scream.

The father turned to see that the petrel-spirit was behind them. It was flying fast. Faster than he could paddle. As he watched, it kept changing shape in mid-air. Its body seemed to stream like smoke. Its wings spread out like angry clouds.

The spirit let out a terrible roar.

Faster and faster, the father's paddle stroked at the water. His breath came in desperate gasps. Despite the chilly sea air, sweat streamed down his face and neck.

But every time he turned to look, the spirit was closer.

Something in the father snapped with panic. How could he stand any more of

this? If only his daughter had accepted a proper husband in the first place! But no, she had to have a stone-turned-dog as a husband—and that had resulted in monster children. And now, her latest husband—a new monster—was bearing down on them.

Was he to let her foolishness kill them both?

No!

With a roar, the father pushed his daughter off the qajaq. She was startled, eyes wide, as she rolled into the frigid water. Still, her hands shot out and grasped the edge of the boat.

"Father!" she cried.

The father watched his daughter for a moment. Their terrified gazes locked. Then the father glanced at the angry spirit, still streaming through the sky at him.

Pulling out his knife, the father cut at his daughter's fingers. She clung, crying out at each blow. Blood streamed from her hands. But still, she would not let go.

The father bared his teeth and kept cutting. His terror lent him strength. Within seconds, pieces of his daughter's fingers came away. First, her fingertips, nails and all, were gone.

The father struck her again.

The next joints of her hands came away. As did her thumbs. The man watched as pieces of his daughter were washed away by the cold water.

Once there was nothing left to grip with, the daughter sank. The last thing the father saw of his daughter was her gaze:

her look of betrayal, and her hatred
toward him.

He turned and paddled to safety.

That girl did not die, however. The world
is full of many powers. And they came to
her, attracted by her sadness and rage.
Such powers gathered all around her.
They changed the fingerless girl. They
even changed the pieces of her fingers,
left to float and drift in the sea. Some of
the finger bits became living seals. Others
became whales. All the parts of the girl's
hands became all the mammals of the sea.

Through the mysteries of the world's
powers, the girl's hatred made her
powerful. Though she had no fingers,
no thumbs, she could still control the
animals that had been created from her
hands. She was a woman now—not a
girl—and would never again live among
human beings. She hated humankind. All

people, as she saw it, were like her father: fearful and selfish.

In time, Inuit grew to fear this woman. Generations of Inuit named her in many ways—and one of these names was Nuliajuk.

Nuliajuk used her powers, her spirit-helpers, to watch human beings from below the waves. Their stupidity, their evil treatment of each other, made her howl with rage. And when Nuliajuk grew angry enough, she kept the sea mammals from the people. She hid them away until the people sent a shaman to visit her. And only if that shaman was strong enough, brave enough, could he soothe Nuliajuk, so that hunters could hunt again.

KAUGJAGJUK

*In times long ago:*

A brother and sister went hunting with their family on the sea ice. But the ice broke up. By the time someone noticed an ice pan carrying the boy and girl away, it was too late. No one could do anything but watch as they drifted.

And drifted.

The wind and water carried the brother and sister far from their family—far from any known lands. The two were sure that they would die. But the ice pan eventually floated to a strange coast. There, the boy and girl were found by very cruel people.

Those people kept the children alive,
though barely. They kept them as slaves.

The girl was very good at braiding, so
she was made to braid sinews for the
entire camp. And she lived apart from
her brother. He was made to do only the
dirtiest tasks for people in the camp—
such as emptying containers full of urine.

The boy came to be known as Kaugjagjuk,
because people found it fun to *kaujuk*
him. This meant that they tortured him
by putting their fingers in his nose, lifting
until his nostrils were stretched wide.
Kaugjagjuk was small. He was weak.
He could do nothing to keep people from
bullying him.

When his day's chores were finished,
Kaugjagjuk lived with the dogs. He ate
only what scraps the dogs could not finish.
At night, the dogs kept him warm. They
slept together near the openings to homes,
so that they could get what little warmth

they might find. The people of the camp did not consider Kaugjagjuk to be one of them anyway. So it seemed fitting that, while they laughed and ate and danced to drums, he lay shivering with the animals.

Years passed, and it came to be that Kaugjagjuk had two dogs that he preferred to sleep with. They were quite old, and he called them Pillow and Mattress. Perhaps they were not normal dogs—because he could understand them when they spoke. And they could understand him.

One winter night, when there was a great full moon, Kaugjagjuk was awakened by the sound of a man's voice. It called, "Kaugjagjuk! Kaugjagjuk! Come out!"

But Kaugjagjuk, eyes wide with fear, stayed in the iglu entranceway. He looked at the dog he called Pillow, then said, "Go and see who it is!"

Pillow went out to do as Kaugjagjuk had asked. But soon the old dog came back in. He told Kaugjagjuk that there was nothing to see, and to go back to sleep.

Sometime later, the voice called again.

"Kaugjagjuk! Kaugjagjuk! Come out!"

This time the boy sent Mattress. The old dog went out, and came back saying the same thing as Pillow: there was nothing; go to sleep.

When the voice called a third time, Kaugjagjuk finally decided to see

for himself. He crawled out of the
entranceway, and saw nothing at first.
Then the light of the full moon caught
his eye. He turned and drew a startled
breath.

A tall man was framed against the moon's
silver glow. He carried a spear. And a
whip. His grim eyes were locked upon
Kaugjagjuk, who cringed at the man's
feet.

Who was this man? To this day, some
claim that it was Kaugjagjuk's uncle, a
powerful shaman. Others claim that it
was Kaugjagjuk's older brother, who had
used his magic powers to stay invisible in
the camp. Still others claim that it was
the spirit of the moon itself—*Taqqiup
Inua*—who sometimes takes pity on those
who suffer.

So, Kaugjagjuk had been called out by the
Moon.

The Moon Man began to walk. Kaugjagjuk followed. Though it was cold, Kaugjagjuk followed the Moon Man far inland, until they arrived at some high hills. There, the Moon Man led the boy up among windswept ridges, where huge rocks lay crusted in ice and snow.

"You live like a dog," the Moon Man told Kaugjagjuk, "so you are treated like a dog. But I am here to teach you strength."

The boy did not understand. Nor did he understand when the Moon Man pointed to a large rock, saying, "Lift it."

The Moon Man barked out his command yet again, and Kaugjagjuk sprang to grab the stone. He grunted, trying with all his might. But the rock would not budge.

"Try harder!" roared the Moon Man.

Kaugjagjuk tried again. He failed again.

Then the Moon Man uncoiled his whip. He

lashed the boy with it.

"You live like a dog," the Moon repeated, "so you are treated like one!"

The whip frightened Kaugjagjuk, so he wrenched at the rock with new strength.

And he lifted it!

The Moon Man led Kaugjagjuk back to

the camp. But he returned the next night. That night, he lashed at the boy once again, until Kaugjagjuk picked up a large stone. This time, the stone was much bigger than what he had lifted the night before.

Many nights followed. Each time, the Moon Man made Kaugjagjuk lift bigger and bigger stones. In time, Kaugjagjuk could lift much more than any normal man. There came a night when he at last lifted the largest boulder on the hilltop. He raised it to the night sky—a boulder so large that it shaded all but his legs from the moon's silver light.

"You are ready," said the Moon Man, smiling grimly.

Once Kaugjagjuk had put the boulder down, the Moon Man told him, "Listen carefully. Go back to your camp. Hide yourself. Three great bears will come to camp, seeking food. They will not be normal bears. Do not show yourself at first. But once the camp folk see the bears . . . well, you will know what to do."

Kaugjagjuk had learned to trust the Moon Man. He did exactly as he was told, returning to camp, then hiding himself with great care. He had not only learned strength, but also patience. He waited for the special bears to arrive.

For long hours, Kaugjagjuk waited. Then long howls—the sound of camp dogs— went up on the wind. They were sounds of alarm, and Kaugjagjuk knew that the bears had arrived.

Soon, the men and women of the camp were scrambling out of their homes, crying out at the sight of the bears. And within minutes, Kaugjagjuk could hear many of them laughing. They were pointing at the approaching bears, saying, "Where is that

Kaugjagjuk? Let's throw him to the bears.
It'll be fun to watch him get eaten."

On hearing these words, rage flared in
Kaugjagjuk's heart. He dashed out of his
hiding place and seized the latest man
who had laughed at the idea of him being
eaten. Kaugjagjuk's new strength was
greater than even he expected. He lifted
the man like an old boot, and flung him
far. The man—no longer laughing, but
screaming—landed near one of the bears.
The huge beast raced over to the man and
bit down on his face. In seconds, it was
eating him alive.

Kaugjagjuk did not pause to watch.
Instead, he caught another man and flung
him to a second bear. Then there was a
third.

Gathering their wits, some of the camp
folk attacked Kaugjagjuk. But their blows
had no effect on him. Instead, he raced

about, catching one person after another.
The bears ate and ate, but never seemed
to grow full. Men and women alike were
thrown to the giant beasts, which were
now red with the blood of dozens.

Kaugjagjuk knew each man, each
woman, whom he threw to the bears. He
remembered everything that every person
had done to him over the years. Every
slap. Every scratch. Every pull of his hair.
He remembered each time that someone
had gouged at his nostrils, pulling him
up like some kind of fish they had caught,
saying things like,

"Useless orphan."
"Less than nothing."
"One of the dogs."

Every time Kaugjagjuk caught someone,
he reminded that person of what they had
done to him, before throwing them to a
bear.

But, strong as he was, there were many people to throw. Kaugjagjuk grew tired. Then he grew less angry. Only when there were four women left did he stop throwing camp folk to the devouring bears.

The bears, however, came after the remaining women.

Kaugjagjuk was exhausted. But he did not want the bears to eat everybody. So he threw himself in front of the bears. He seized them. He wrestled them. And one by one, he tossed the great beasts out of the camp.

Panting, his strength having been tested to its limit, Kaugjagjuk rose and brushed the snow from his clothing. After that time, he lived with the remaining women. Some people say that, among those

MOHLER
2007

women, there were two who had been a
bit kind to him—but there were another
two who had been especially cruel. These,
he kept as his wives. And he was very
cruel to them. No one knows what became
of Kaugjagjuk's sister.

So it was that, with no kindness shown to
him, Kaugjagjuk could show no kindness
to others.

NANURLUK

*In times long ago:*

There was a hunter who was desperate.
He and his young wife had travelled
to new, strange lands. Along the way,
there had been good enough hunting to
keep them both alive. But now, luck had
turned for the worse. If the hunter did
not catch something soon, he and his wife
would be reduced to eating their boots. So,
once more, the hunter set out from their
little home, hoping to bring home a seal.

The wind howled as the hunter made his
way across the sea ice. His eyes looked
everywhere for some sign of an *aglu*—a
seal's ice-domed breathing hole. There

was nothing. As he trudged along, the hunter tried to remember his ancestors. He tried to bear in mind that they had lived through so much worse. Under his breath, he quietly sang the song of his grandfather.

This time, the hunter walked in a different direction. And it was not long before he discovered something odd on the sea ice. He found a raised ridge of ice: a kind of shape in the frozen sea that he had never before seen. As he approached it, he quickly realized that he was looking at a hole in the ice.

And it was huge.

The hunter was puzzled. There was a reason for everything to be. Why was there such a large hole here? As he watched, he saw bubbles rise and break the surface of the hole's dark water.

He leaned over the edge and peered into the hole.

And gasped at what he saw.

Below him, floating underwater, he saw a great white shape. He was looking at fur! It took him only moments to realize that he was seeing a polar bear. But this was no ordinary *nanuq*. This bear was massive—a monster—many times the size of the hunter's own snow house. It was curled like a newborn animal. The hunter could see that its eyes were closed. Black claws, larger than spear tips, were placed over much of the monster's face.

The bear was alive. The hunter was certain of that. The bubbles breaking the water's surface were from the creature's breath.

It seemed that it was asleep.

The hunter shuddered. Then he carefully stepped back from the hole's edge. He guessed that he had been lucky that his footsteps had not already awakened the bear.

What was this thing? The hunter thought about stories that elders had told him. Some, including those told by his own grandfather, had mentioned a creature called the *nanurluk*. This was a bear so huge that it could not live for long on land. Instead, the sea supported its weight. The hunter remembered a story about how such a bear had been killed, long ago. The monster had charged up from the sea, attacking a camp along the shore. But a man had climbed right down its throat, stabbing it from the inside.

He was not about to try that!

Still, the hunter needed to feed his wife. He grew excited, thinking about the meat that he could get off this beast. And the fur!

The hunter thought for a long time. He

worked up his courage. Then, being very,
very quiet, he began to gather snow.

Though it took a long time, the hunter
wetted handfuls of snow in the sea water.
Then he packed the wet snow around the
edge of the nanurluk's breathing hole.

Gather. Wet. Pack. Gather. Wet. Pack.

The labour went on and on, until the
hunter was trembling with effort. But
at last, using the ice that he had made
himself, he narrowed the opening.

Once the hole was much more narrow,
the hunter had to summon his courage
once again. In his head, he sang his
grandfather's song. He straddled the hole.

His knife was in one hand.

His spear was in the other.

Then something went wrong.

The hunter's shadow fell on the hole. The change in light seemed to startle the bear. Its great eyes snapped open beneath the water, and the bear surged upward before the hunter had a chance to pull back his spear.

The hunter saw a great black nose.

Too fast! It was coming too fast!

There was an explosion of ice and water as the bear broke through the hole. The hunter managed only to slash at the bear's nose with his knife, before he was sent flying. He rolled and rolled, covered in sea water. Wet chunks of ice rained down on him, striking his head, dazing him. He fought to get back up onto his feet.

But he had lost his weapons!

The hunter turned to see the bear's head,

and the leading edges of its paws, sticking
out of the ice. The nanurluk seemed
to be stuck. The creature's nose was
bleeding, but it was otherwise healthy.
The hunter turned pale as the monster
eyed him and let loose a roar that shook
the surrounding ice. In that moment, its
breath was like hot wind. He could see the
black tongue curling in its open mouth.
He could see its teeth. They were as long
as his arms. He was close enough that, if
he had wanted, he could have counted the
chips in them.

But the bear, he realized, could not reach
him. As the hunter stood watching, its
shoulders twisted and wrenched at the
ice.

Slipping, sliding in a spray of water,
the hunter fumbled for his spear. The
knife was gone, but the spear—his most
important weapon—had landed nearby.

The nanurluk fought to free itself. It

twisted and surged forward again. This
time, the ice began to crack.

Gripping his spear tightly, the hunter ran
at the monster. He stabbed at its most
sensitive spots: its eyes. Within seconds,
there was blood all along the length of the
hunter's spear—on the hunter himself
up to his elbows—and the nanurluk was
blinded.

Whether in fury or panic, upon having its
eyes attacked the giant bear gave a last
heave. It broke free from the surrounding
ice, and the hunter was once again thrown
backward. The hunter watched, feeling
helpless, as the monster dragged its
wet body up onto the sea ice. The water
gushing off its pelt sounded like the roar
of a waterfall.

The hunter stood back up, still gripping
his spear. He was soaked. He was out of
breath. If the great jaws came to snap him

up like a snack, there was little he could
do about it.

The bear, however, did not attack. It
chuffed loudly, panting, turning in all
directions. Blood streamed from its nose
and eyes. It seemed to be searching for the
hunter. But it could not see him. And—
perhaps with the scent of blood filling its
nostrils—it could not smell him, either.

The hunter grew hopeful. Maybe if he
stood still, the beast would not find him.

Yet the hunter's relief turned to fear. As
he watched, the bear lumbered off in the
direction of the hunter's own home.

His wife!

He had hoped to feed her. But what if she
were eaten by the very creature that he
had intended to feed her with? The hunter
was terrified, but he needed to know if the

nanurluk found his home. Maybe there was a chance that he could yell out to his wife, warn her . . .

As soon as he was sure that it was safe to move—since he did not want to make too much noise—the hunter began to follow the bear. Being wet, he shivered. But he forced himself to put one foot before the next, following the bear's bloody trail.

He fell behind, until the monster was far ahead of him.

In time, the hunter followed the red trail over a low slope, and his snow house was within sight. So was the bear. But the monster now lay still. Just within sight of the hunter's home, the nanurluk had died. As it had walked, its blood had streamed out behind it, until life had at last left the beast.

The hunter gasped with relief as his wife

rushed out to meet him. She helped him recover. And that very night, they ate bear meat. For the first time in a long while, the husband and wife laughed together. Their worries were forgotten. The hunter sang his grandfather's song out loud. And there was food and fur for many days to come.

# UNDERSTANDING
## INUIT
## LEGENDS
## &
## LORE

Inuit have often been depicted as a joyful folk, mostly because of their tendency to be mild, welcoming, and ready to laugh.

There was great happiness in the old days. But not because life was easy. The Land was, and is, harsh. There was famine. Murder. Evil. If Inuit had developed love for the sunnier side of existence, so to speak, it was because the Land filled life with many hard winters.

The question has often been asked: if Inuit are mild in their day-to-day behaviours, why are their stories so horrific?

An answer lies in the fact that Inuit tended to respect each other's *isuma*,

the thoughts and feelings particular to
an individual. While there were codes of
behaviour, it was considered bad manners
(at the very least) to dictate behaviour
to another. Inuit were an action-oriented
people. They tended to reject theories as
empty notions that go round and round
in one's head. They embraced knowledge
that achieved practical ends.

A problem, then: can one even teach a
moral lesson, when it is rude to simply
tell another how to behave?

This problem was solved with "cautionary
tales." These were stories held up as
examples, not of noble deeds but of
breakdowns in societal values and
morality. Inuit learned, then, by learning
what not to do.

Take, for example, the story of Nuliajuk.
Inhabit Media asked us to present it in
especially simple form, for the sake of this
short work. But it is really a very detailed
and ancient tale, with links to the entire
circumpolar world. The girl who refuses

to marry goes by many names, only one
of which is Nuliajuk. It is often told as
two separate stories (one concerning
her marriage to a dog, in which she is
known as Uinigumasuittuq; the other
as kidnapped bride, or Nuliajuk —in
English, Sedna).

This is a highly moralistic tale. It seems
to be about a stubborn girl, which it is,
but it more strictly concerns her father.
Most problems, if one looks closely, stem
from his insistence that she follow his
wishes (that is, finds a man). It is not as
much the nasty bird-monster that violates
her, as her own father, who violates her
isuma. His final act—chopping off her
fingers to abandon her—is a betrayal
more monstrous than anything she suffers
under an inhuman creature.

Nuliajuk's wrath, then, is justified; and
it is no accident that, forever after, she
rages in answer to the sins of humankind.
Her own pain, in the end, causes her
to become a supernatural avenger. No
longer are humankind's sins allowed to go

unanswered. Her wrath can now starve humanity.

The story of Kaugjagjuk is even more obviously cautionary—a statement against the mistreatment of orphans, which is a common theme in Inuit lore. This is a tale of injustice but also of starkest terror. Since Inuit depended on one another to hunt, so that they construct clothing and shelters in order to live at all, the threat of abandonment was the worst scenario that one could face. How can we feel for this evil community when Kaugjagjuk feeds them to bears? They subjected Kaugjagjuk to the worst of all social terrors. Kaugjagjuk's answer, when he gains power, is to feed them to that very beast which terrified Inuit for millennia—the polar bear.

The bear recurs in the last story, as a supernatural creature that Inuit most often called Nanurluk. This bear, which some elders call a spirit, is not rampaging, but simply asleep under the ice. This tale is not really about the bear but about

the pride of the hunter who wants it. It
is a caution against excessive hunger,
excessive greed, and excessive ambition.
The hunter escapes, but just barely, and
almost at the cost of his beloved wife.
This story holds one of the few happy
endings in Inuit lore, yet it carries the
caution that danger occurs in proportion
to craving.

These stories all present different
characters and events, while a common
essence runs through them: wrath
in Nuliajuk, fear in Kaugjagjuk, and
craving in the Nanurluk tale. This is
unsurprising. For wrath, fear, and hunger
are all aspects of what Inuit call *uumaniq*.
This means life in its most raw, animal
form, involving nothing of awareness
or spiritual qualities. These tales, in
other words, caution against unchecked
instincts. Instincts, undisciplined, make
man no better than a beast.

The stories, in other words, are a
reminder to stay human.

## RACHEL AND SEAN QITSUALIK-TINSLEY

Born in an Arctic wilderness camp and of Inuit ancestry, Rachel Qitsualik-Tinsley is a scholar specializing in world religions and cultures. Her numerous articles and books concerning Inuit magic and lore have earned her a Queen Elizabeth II Diamond Jubilee Medal.

Of Scottish-Mohawk ancestry, Sean Qitsualik-Tinsley is a folklorist and fantasist, specializing in mythology, magic, and Inuit lore. He has won an award for writing short science fiction ("Green Angel"), but his focus is on fiction and non-fiction for a young audience.

JEREMY MOHLER

Jeremy read his first comic book in middle school. From that day forward, he devoted himself to art. He attended the Joe Kubert School of Cartoon and Graphic Art and earned his BFA from the Kansas City Art Institute. In 2008, Jeremy founded Outland Entertainment to help clients bring their projects to life. Since its inception, Outland has helped more than one hundred companies and individuals to develop ideas into full-fledged, finished products. He currently lives in Topeka, Kansas, with his wife and two daughters.

# ABOUT
# INHABIT MEDIA INC.

Inhabit Media Inc. is an Inuit-owned publishing company located in Iqaluit, Nunavut, Canada. We are the only independent publishing company located in the eastern Arctic of Canada. We have been working since 2006 to ensure that Inuit stories and oral history are recorded and preserved for future generation.

Inhabit Media believes that it is important that the North is represented by the people who live there, and that their stories have a place in the larger world of publishing.

If you are interested in northern stories or Inuit culture, please visit our website:

www.inhabitmedia.com

# ALSO RECOMMENDED
## OTHER BOOKS ABOUT ARCTIC FOLKLORE
## THAT YOU MIGHT ENJOY

"*Skraelings* takes readers through a quick and exciting adventure in the Arctic at the time of Viking exploration . . . a thoughtful and unique story of the north."
— *Canadian Review of Materials*

"*Skraelings* is a well-written, engaging introduction to the complex history of the peoples of the Arctic and their struggles for survival against the environment and each other."
— *School Library Journal*

Nominated for the 2013 Silver Birch Award and the 2014 Rocky Mountain Book Award.

"*The Shadows That Rush Past* is an important contribution to Inuit and Canadian lore."
— *Canadian Review of Materials*

INHABIT

M E D I A